This book
belongs to

Linda McGregor
Sunshine Nursery

D1328966

Other books by Mick Inkpen:

KIPPER
KIPPER'S TOYBOX
KIPPER'S BIRTHDAY
KIPPER'S BOOK OF COLOURS
KIPPER'S BOOK OF COUNTING
KIPPER'S BOOK OF WEATHER
ONE BEAR AT BEDTIME
THE BLUE BALLOON
THREADBEAR
BILLY'S BEETLE
PENGUIN SMALL
LULLABYHULLABALLOO!
WIBBLY PIG BOARD BOOKS
NOTHING

British Library Cataloguing in Publication Data

A catalogue record for this book is available
from the British Library

ISBN 0 340 63483 9



First published 1994
First paperback edition 1996
10 9 8 7 6 5 4 3 2 1

Published by Hodder Children's Books,
a division of Hodder Headline plc,
338 Euston Road, London NW1 3BH

Printed in Italy by L.E.G.O., Vicenza

# *KIPPER'S BOOK OF* OPPOSITES

*Mick Inkpen*

Hodder Children's Books
a division of Hodder Headline plc

New

# Old

# Out

# In

Happy

# Sad

Up

Down

# Slow

Fast

# Long

# Short

# Big

# Small

# Day

# Night